TIM BURTON

THE NIGHTMARE BEFORE CHRISTMAS

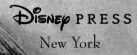 PRESS

New York

Acknowledgments

With thanks to:
Lisa Marie, Diane Minter, Jill Jacobs,
Virgil Young, Wendy Breck, Jesyca Durchin,
Michael Lynton, Andrea Cascardi, Ellen Friedman

Text and illustrations © 1993 by Tim Burton
All rights reserved
Printed in Singapore
For information address Disney Press,
114 Fifth Avenue, New York, New York 10011.
4th Edition
5 7 9 10 8 6 4

Library of Congress Catalog Card Number: 2005928135

ISBN 10: 0-7868-4908-8

ISBN 13: 978-0-7868-4908-6

This book is set in 18-point Bernhard Modern.

THE NIGHTMARE BEFORE CHRISTMAS

It was late one fall in Halloweenland, and the air had quite a chill.
Against the moon a skeleton sat, alone upon a hill.
He was tall and thin with a bat bow tie;
Jack Skellington was his name.
He was tired and bored in Halloweenland —
Everything was always the same.

"I'm sick of the scaring, the terror, the fright.
I'm tired of being something that goes bump in the night.
I'm bored with leering my horrible glances,
And my feet hurt from dancing those skeleton dances.
I don't like graveyards, and I need something new.
There must be more to life than just yelling, 'Boo!'"

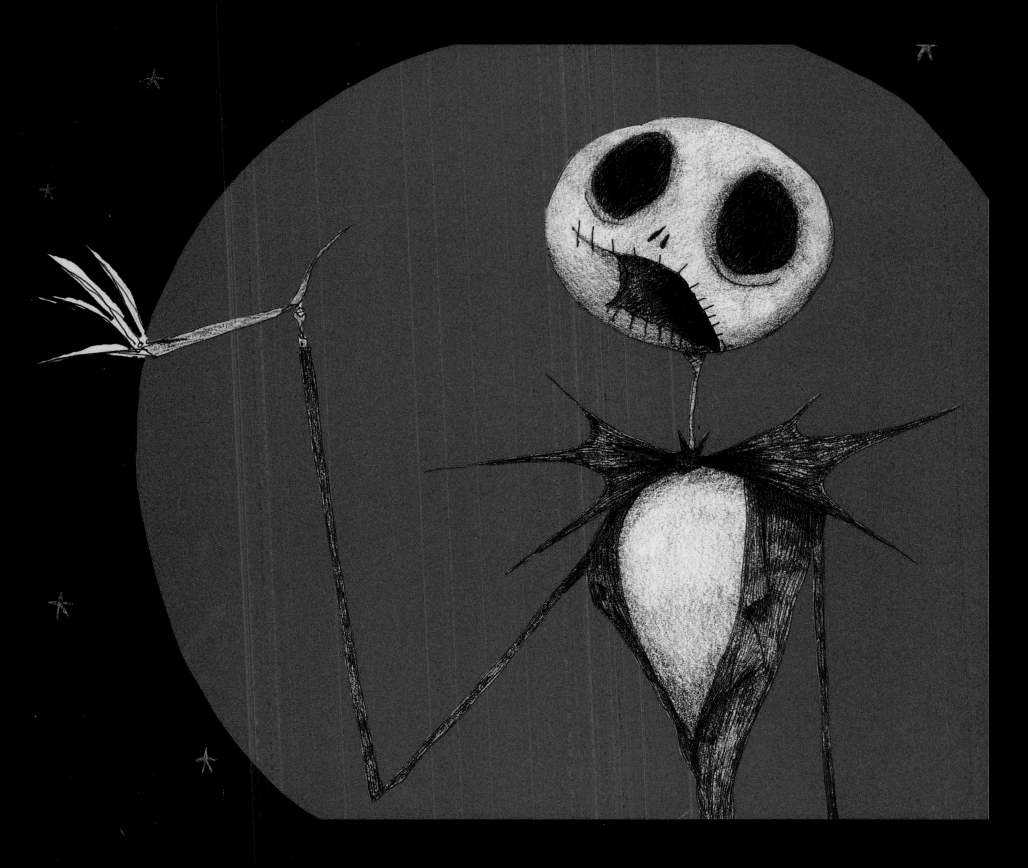

Then out from the grave, with a curl and a twist,
Came a whimpering, whining, spectral mist.
It was a little ghost dog with a faint little bark,
And a jack-o'-lantern nose that glowed in the dark.
It was Jack's dog, Zero, the best friend he had,
But Jack hardly noticed, which made Zero sad.

All that night and through the next day,
Jack wandered and walked. He was filled with dismay.

Then deep in the forest, just before night,
Jack came upon an amazing sight.
Not twenty feet from the spot where he stood
Were three massive doorways carved in wood.
He stood before them, completely in awe,
His gaze transfixed by one special door.
Entranced and excited, with a slight sense of worry,
Jack opened the door to a white, windy flurry.

Jack didn't know it, but he'd fallen down
In the middle of a place called Christmas Town!

Immersed in the light, Jack was no longer haunted.
He had finally found the feeling he wanted.
And so that his friends wouldn't think him a liar,
He took the present-filled stockings that hung by the fire.
He took candy and toys that were stacked on the shelves
And a picture of Santa with all of his elves.
He took lights and ornaments and the star from the tree,
And from the Christmas Town sign, he took the big letter C.

He picked up everything that sparkled or glowed.
He even picked up a handful of snow.
He grabbed it all, and without being seen,
He took it all back to Halloween.

Back in Halloween a group of Jack's peers
Stared in amazement at his Christmas souvenirs.
For this wondrous vision none were prepared.
Most were excited, though a few were quite scared!

For the next few days, while it lightninged and thundered,
Jack sat alone and obsessively wondered.
"Why is it they get to spread laughter and cheer
While we stalk the graveyards, spreading panic and fear?
Well, *I* could be Santa, and *I* could spread cheer!
Why does *he* get to do it year after year?"
Outraged by injustice, Jack thought and he thought.
Then he got an idea. "Yes...yes...why not!"

In Christmas Town, Santa was making some toys
When through the din he heard a soft noise.
He answered the door, and to his surprise,
He saw weird little creatures in strange disguise.
They were altogether ugly and rather petite.
As they opened their sacks, they yelled, "Trick or treat!"
Then a confused Santa was shoved into a sack
And taken to Halloween to see mastermind Jack.

In Halloween everyone gathered once more,
For they'd never seen a Santa before.

And as they cautiously gazed at this strange old man,
Jack related to Santa his masterful plan:
"My dear Mr. Claus, I think it's a crime
That you've got to be Santa all of the time!
But now *I* will give presents, and *I* will spread cheer.
We're changing places — I'm Santa this year.
It is *I* who will say Merry Christmas to you!
So you may lie in my coffin, creak doors, and yell, 'Boo!'
And please, Mr. Claus, don't think ill of my plan.
For I'll do the best Santa job that I can."

And though Jack and his friends thought they'd do a good job,
Their idea of Christmas was still quite macabre.

They were packed up and ready on Christmas Eve day
When Jack hitched his reindeer to his sleek coffin sleigh,
But on Christmas Eve as they were about to begin,
A Halloween fog slowly rolled in.
Jack said, "We can't leave; this fog's just too thick.
There will be no Christmas, and I can't be St. Nick."
Then a small glowing light pierced through the fog.
What could it be?...It was Zero, Jack's dog!

Jack said, "Zero, with your nose so bright,
Won't you guide my sleigh tonight?"

And to be so needed was Zero's great dream,
So he joyously flew to the head of the team.
And as the skeletal sleigh started its ghostly flight,
Jack cackled, "Merry Christmas to all, and to all a good night!"

'Twas the nightmare before Christmas, and all through the house,
Not a creature was peaceful, not even a mouse.
The stockings, all hung by the chimney with care,
When opened that morning would cause quite a scare!
The children, all nestled so snug in their beds,
Would have nightmares of monsters and skeleton heads.
The moon that hung over the new-fallen snow
Cast an eerie pall over the city below,
And Santa Claus's laughter now sounded like groans,
And the jingling bells like chattering bones.
And what to their wondering eyes should appear,
But a coffin sleigh with skeleton deer.
And a skeletal driver so ugly and sick
They knew in a moment, this can't be St. Nick!
From house to house, with a true sense of joy,
Jack happily issued each present and toy.
From rooftop to rooftop he jumped and he skipped,
Leaving presents that seemed to be straight from a crypt!
Unaware that the world was in panic and fear,
Jack merrily spread his own brand of cheer.

He visited the house of Susie and Dave;
They got a Gumby and Pokey from the grave.
Then on to the home of little Jane Neeman;
She got a baby doll possessed by a demon.

A monstrous train with tentacle tracks,
A ghoulish puppet wielding an ax,

A man-eating plant disguised as a wreath,
And a vampire teddy bear with very sharp teeth.

There were screams of terror, but Jack didn't hear it,
He was much too involved with his own Christmas spirit!
Jack finally looked down from his dark, starry frights
And saw the commotion, the noise, and the lights.
"Why, they're celebrating, it looks like such fun!
They're thanking me for the good job that I've done."
But what he thought were fireworks meant as goodwill
Were bullets and missiles intended to kill.
Then amidst the barrage of artillery fire,
Jack urged Zero to go higher and higher.
And away they all flew like the storm of a thistle
Until they were hit by a well-guided missile.
And as they fell on the cemetery, way out of sight,
Was heard, "Merry Christmas to all, and to all a good night."

Jack pulled himself up on a large stone cross,
And from there he reviewed his incredible loss.
"I thought I could be Santa, I had such belief..."
Jack was confused and filled with great grief.
Not knowing where to turn, he looked toward the sky,
Then he slumped on the grave and he started to cry.
And as Zero and Jack lay crumpled on the ground,
They suddenly heard a familiar sound....

"My dear Jack," said Santa, "I applaud your intent.
I know wreaking such havoc was not what you meant.
And so you are sad and feeling quite blue,
But taking over Christmas was the wrong thing to do.
I hope you realize Halloween's the right place for you.
There's a lot more, Jack, that I'd like to say,
But now I must hurry, for it's almost Christmas day."

Then he jumped in his sleigh, and with a wink of an eye,
He said, "Merry Christmas," and he bid them good-bye.

Back home, Jack was sad,
but then, like a dream,
Santa brought Christmas
to the land of Halloween.

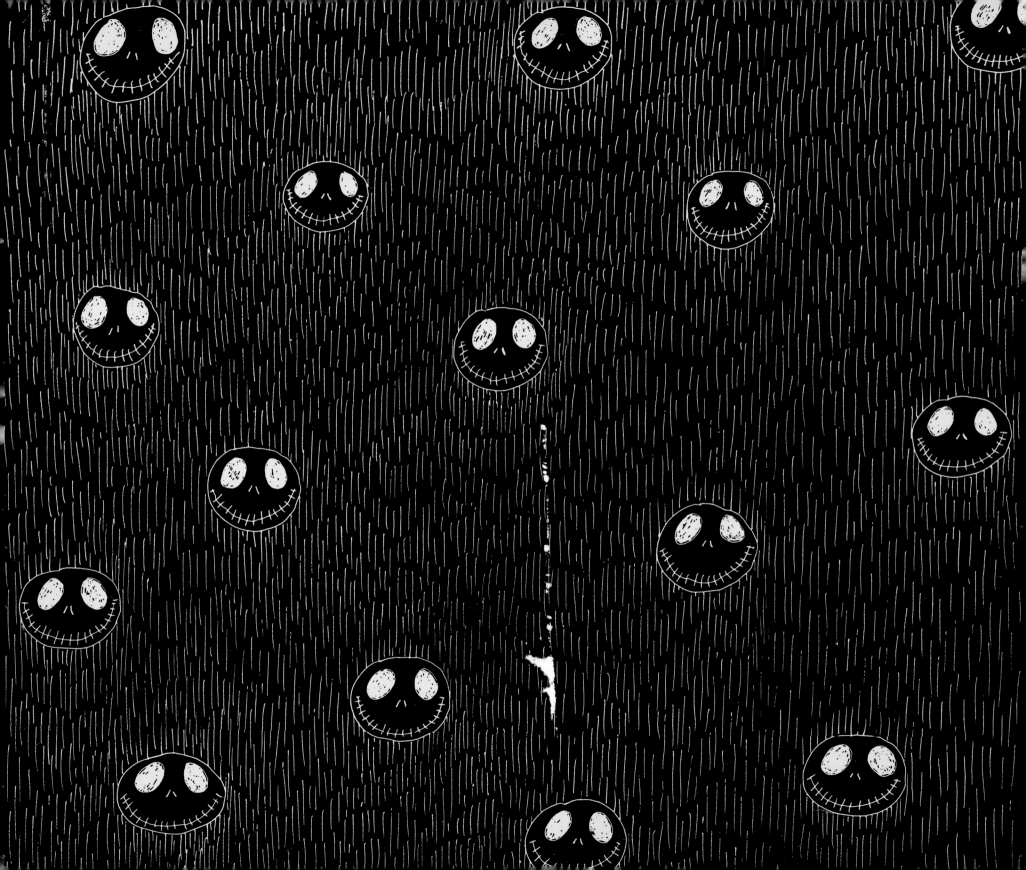